To

James,

Love from

....

I love you dearly,

James,

and I love to watch you grow.

Each day you bring me far more joy
than you could ever know.

James,
I love your sleepy eyes,
in the early start of day.

Your face is who I want to see
so we can run and play.

James,
I love to see you giggle
when you're jumping on my bed.

To see your little dimples
as you laugh at what I've said.

James,

I love the little noises that
you make each time you eat.

Taking tiny nibbles,
on a yummy, tasty treat.

James,

I love your curiosity
as you discover and explore.

Watching your mind blossom,
into something so much more.

James,
I love it when you're kind,
you're so thoughtful and so smart.

Working together with your friends,
you have such a caring heart.

James,

I love those little games
you create, learn, and play.

I'm your biggest fan,
I'll forever feel this way.

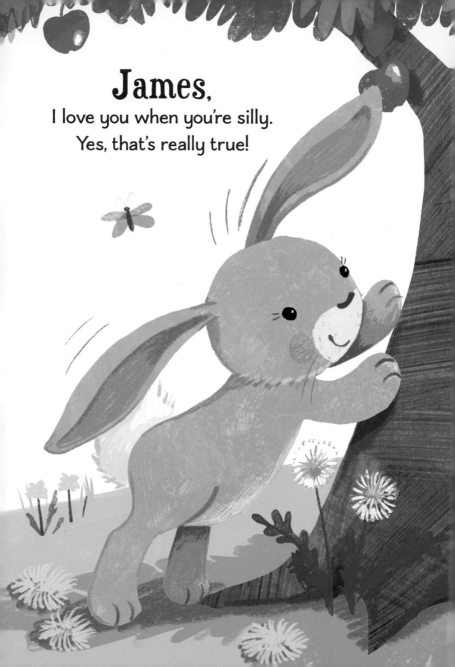

James,
I love you when you're silly.
Yes, that's really true!

You are so very funny
in everything you do.

James,

I love that look of joy when
you get bubbles in your hair.

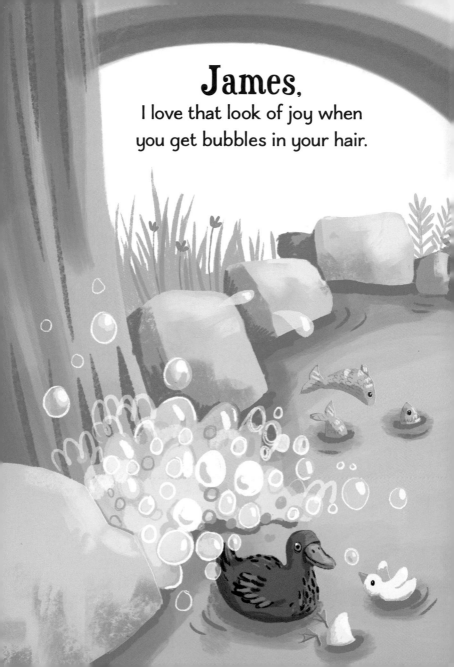

Even when you're splashing
lots of water everywhere!

James,

I love it when you share,
your stories and your dreams.

Spending time together,
counting stars and moonbeams.

James,

I love your little sleepy face
when you begin to yawn.

I can't wait to see your smile again
in the early dawn.

James,
I love everything you say
and all the things you do.

But most of all I love you
just for being YOU!

All the things
I love about
James.

James,

draw a picture of the things that you love!

Written by J.D. Green
Illustrated by Joanne Partis
Designed by Ryan Dunn

Copyright © Bidu Bidu Books Ltd. 2020

Published by Put Me In The Story,
a publication of Sourcebooks.
P.O. Box 4410, Naperville, Illinois 60567-4410
(630) 536-1104
putmeinthestory.com

Date of Production: August 2022
Run Number: 5027269
Printed and bound in China (GD)
10 9 8 7 6 5 4

MIX
Paper from
responsible sources
FSC® C117745

put me in the story
Bestselling books starring your child!
putmeinthestory.com